My Grandma's Party

Illustrations by
Priscilla Lamont

First published in Great Britain 2000 by Egmont Children's Books Limited
239 Kensington High Street, London W8 6SA
Illustrated by Priscilla Lamont
Text by Susan Hitches. Designed by Mandy Norman.
Copyright © 2000 Egmont Children's Books Limited
ISBN 0 7497 4189 9
Printed in Italy

1 3 5 7 9 10 8 6 4 2

"Good night, Jack. Sleep tight!" says Mum. "It's Grandma's party tomorrow. We'll get up early to bake some cakes."

"Grandma's coming at tea time," says Mum.
"The party is a surprise for her. Let's finish
breakfast and start work on the cakes."

"You could draw a picture of the cat. Grandma likes her," says Mum. "Auntie is coming over soon to help, too."

"We need to make lots of little cakes," says Mum.
"Don't get too much mixture on the table."

"Hello, Jack," says Auntie. "Those cakes look delicious. Can I eat one now?"

"Let's finish the decorations for Grandma's party. Can you blow up another balloon?" says Auntie.

"I hope we're ready on time," says Mum.

"Hello, everyone. Come in," says Mum.
"This is a lovely surprise!" says Grandma.

"Up you come," says Grandpa. "Look at all those candles for Grandma!"

"Will you help me blow out the candles?"
says Grandma. "One, two, three . . ."

"Let Grandma open the first present," says Mum.
"You can open another one for her."

"I love my presents," says Grandma.
"Thank you, everyone."

"It's the best birthday card I've ever seen,"
says Grandma. "Thank you, Jack."

"I'll read you all a story," says Gran.
"But you'll have to hold the book for me.
Wasn't it a lovely party?"